The Tiger and the General

Published by Treasure Tower Books
The children's book division of the SGI-USA
606 Wilshire Blvd., Santa Monica, CA 90401
© 2007 SGI-USA

ISBN 978-1-932911-32-9

Cover and interior design by SunDried Penguin Design

10 9 8 7 6 5 4 3 2 1

A long time ago, there lived in China a general named Li Kuang.

He was a very strong and brave general.

As soon as enemy soldiers saw his face, they would shake with fear and race away.

"Run! It's General Li Kuang! Let's get out of here!" they yelled.

But Li Kuang was also kind-hearted and loved his mother and father very much.

"Mother, dear, let me rub your shoulders," he said.

"Here, Father, let me chop that wood for you," he said.

All the people in his village praised Li Kuang and admired him because he was a good son and helped his parents whenever he could.

One day, something terrible happened.

This strong and brave general was seen crying in anguish.

"What happened?" everyone asked.

"Oh, it's horrible!" said Li Kuang. "A tiger has attacked and killed my mother." The general grabbed his bow and arrows. "I'm going to get that tiger if it's the last thing I do!" he shouted through his tears.

From that day on, General Li Kuang could think of nothing except finding the tiger. He swore to avenge his mother's death.

Whenever he glimpsed the tiger, he chased after it, yelling, "Wait until I get my hands on you, you miserable beast!"

Even in the dark and dangerous woods high in the mountains, when the general caught sight of the tiger, he ran after it, thinking of his mother.

But the tiger always heard him coming and escaped, running like the wind.

Gulp, gulp gulp. The tiger lapped water from a small pond in the forest.

The general, following the tiger's trail, caught sight of his quarry drinking.

"Excellent! I found him! This time, he won't get away!"

He crept slowly toward the tiger, moving carefully so as not to make a sound.

But the tiger pricked up his ears. "Oh ho! It's that general again!"

The tiger turned and ran. In the blink of an eye, he escaped into the confusing maze of the forest.

"Wait! Come back, you monster!" General Li Kuang ran as fast as he could, but in no time the tiger was lost in the deep grasses and trees of the forest.

The general was discouraged. But he thought again of his beloved mother and felt his resolve grow strong once again. "No matter what," he said to himself, "I will kill that beast!"

Then suddenly Li Kuang saw something move behind the shadow of the leaves. "What's that?" He peered closely and saw a dark shape.

"It's him! It's the tiger!"

Quickly and silently, the general fixed his sharpest arrow into his bow.

"I've got you now, you miserable beast," he whispered. "Don't move...."

He drew back his powerful bow and let the arrow fly.

Whoosh!

"I got him! I got him!" The general jumped up and down with relief and joy. "I killed the terrible tiger!"

He ran toward the dark shape that was the tiger's body.

When he was close enough to see clearly, General Li Kuang stood still and stared. He was astonished. "What is this?"

Instead of a tiger, he saw a huge rock. Sticking out of the rock was the arrow he had just shot.

He whistled with surprise. "How could my arrow pierce solid rock?"

Thud! Thud! Thud! One after another, the general shot more arrows at the stone.

No matter how hard he tried, the arrows bounced off the solid rock and clattered to the ground.

The general sat puzzling over this. Then suddenly he sprang up.

"Ah hah!" he cried. "I get it! The reason my first arrow lodged in the rock was because I absolutely believed that the rock was my sworn enemy, the terrible tiger. And because my determination to shoot the tiger was as solid as that rock, my arrow pierced it. Well, well, well...."

The story of the general and the tiger spread throughout the village and nearby areas.

"I heard that General Li Kuang shot an arrow at a rock and pierced it," people said.

"Yes," The townspeople said to one another. "When we have a strong desire, a dream, a goal, we can bring out the most amazing strength from within ourselves."

General Li Kuang agreed. "Nothing is impossible for a determined mind," he said. And from then on, General Stone Tiger, as the people called him, was considered a hero.

About This Story

This Chinese folktale teaches us that faith and determination are very powerful. Normally, no one could shoot an arrow into a rock, but Li Kuang was absolutely determined.

Faith in Nam-myoho-renge-kyo can make things happen even when they seem impossible. Nichiren shared the story of General Li Kuang to teach us that when we believe completely in the power of our own lives, our Buddhahood, and chant Nam-myoho-renge-kyo to the Gohonzon, we can do anything.

When we are tired or sad, we may wonder if we can win over our problems or reach our dreams. When we give in to doubt, however, we limit ourselves. When we chant Nam-myoho-renge-kyo, we can see into the unlimited and joyous future that we are creating. Nichiren urges us to use even bad situations, whatever they may be, to strengthen our faith, so that we can always win.

There is a saying, "Nothing is impossible to a determined mind." When we make a promise and we work hard to keep it, we can bring out great courage and strength and wisdom.